ANNA MELICK MEMORIAL SCHOOL
R.R. 8, DUNNVILLE, ONTARIO
N1A 2W7

JAPAN

Richard Tames

Franklin Watts

New York/Chicago/London/Toronto/Sydney

Copyright © 1988, 1994 Franklin Watts

Franklin Watts
95 Madison Avenue
New York, NY 10016

Library of Congress Cataloging-in-Publication Data
Tames, Richard.
   Passport to Japan/Richard Tames.
     p. cm. - (Passport to)
   Includes bibliographical references and index.
   ISBN 0-531-14321-X
   1. Japan. I. Title II. Series
DS806. T2933 1994   93-38981
952–dc20   CIP AC

Editors: John Clark
          Hal Robinson
Design: Edward Kinsey
Illustrations: Hayward Art Group
Consultant: Keith Lye

Photographs: Chris Fairclough Colour Library 19B, 24, 25; Michael Holford 40B, 41B, 42T, 43T; Hutchison Picture Library 5T, 9TL, 9TR, 9CL, 9CR, 9B, 11B, 13B, 16T, 16B, 17, 18T, 22T, 22B, 28B, 41T, 43B, 44BL, 44BR; Japanese Information and Cultural Centre 6T, 6B, 11T, 23T, 29, 30, 33, 45TR, 45B; Popperfoto 44T, 45TL; Richard Tames 21B, 36B, 37, 38T, 40T, 42BL; Tokyo Information Centre 42BR; Zefa Picture Library 5B, 6B, 6T, 8T, 8B, 9TL, 10T, 12T, 13T, 18B, 19T, 20T, 20B, 21T, 23B, 28T, 32T, 32B, 38T, 38B, 39TL, 39TR, 39B.

Front cover: Zefa; Japanese Information and Cultural Centre (inset).

Special thanks are due to the Japan Centre, London, for their help and cooperation.

Printed in Belgium

All rights reserved

Contents

Introduction	5
The land	6
The people	8
Where people live	10
Tokyo	12
Fact file: land and population	14
Home life	16
Stores and shopping	18
Cooking and eating	20
Pastimes and sports	22
News and broadcasting	24
Fact file: home and leisure	26
Farming and fishing	28
Industry	30
Transportation	32
Fact file: economy and trade	34
Education	36
Traditional Japan	38
The arts	40
The making of modern Japan	42
Japan in the modern world	44
Fact file: government and world role	46
Index	48

Introduction

Japan is an island nation in the northeastern Pacific Ocean facing Russia, Korea, and China. There are four main islands – Honshu, which makes up about 60 percent of the country, Hokkaido, Kyushu, and Shikoku – together with thousands of smaller islands, including the Bonin and Ryukyu chains.

Many Japanese thought of their country as "the Britain of Asia," because it had evolved a distinctive character despite its position off the coast of a great continent. But Japan lies about five times as far from the Asian mainland as Britain does from Europe. The Japanese have used the intervening seas as both a bridge and a barrier, welcoming peaceful traders, scholars, diplomats, craftspeople, and missionaries, but stoutly resisting invaders.

However, following its attempts to become the dominant military power in Asia in the 1930s and 1940s, Japan was occupied and many of its cities lay in ruins. After the Allied occupying forces withdrew in 1952, the Japanese people set about rebuilding their shattered economy. They achieved an economic miracle, transforming their country into the world's second largest economy after the United States.

Above: The Asakusa temple, dedicated to Kannon, Buddhist goddess of mercy, is one of the few ancient buildings to survive in central Tokyo.

Below: Twilight in the Ginza, one of Tokyo's main shopping thoroughfares. Notice the signs in English.

The land

Japan's land area is slightly smaller than that of California and somewhat larger than that of Finland. It is scenic country, about three-quarters of which is hilly, with steep slopes covered with forest. The highest peak is Mount Fuji, also called Fujiyama or Fujisan. Situated on Honshu, to the southwest of Tokyo, Mount Fuji is a volcano, which last erupted in 1707.

Japan rests on an extremely unstable part of the Earth's crust. It contains about 200 volcanoes, more than 60 of which are active. Earthquakes are also common, though most do no damage. Severe earthquakes do occur occasionally, however. The world's most destructive earthquake occurred in Japan in 1923, when more than 100,000 people were killed, or missing and presumed dead.

Some powerful earthquakes occur on the seabed, often causing blocks of land to rise or sink. Such earthquakes can generate huge, fast-moving waves called tsunami, which batter coastal areas.

Above: Lakes and sea inlets provide beautiful recreation areas throughout Japan.

Below: Japan has little flat land. Valley floors are intensely farmed with ricefields.

The country has no long rivers, but there are many short, fast-flowing ones. There are many flat coastlands, including the Kanto plain behind Tokyo, but most are small in area. The mostly jagged shoreline of the main islands is about 9,936 miles (16,000 km) long.

The Ryukyu Islands, which run to the southwest of the main islands, are the rugged pinnacles of a submerged mountain range. These islands, the largest of which is Okinawa, contain several active volcanoes. The smaller Bonin Islands, south of Tokyo, are also volcanic.

Superimposed on a map of the United States, the islands of Japan would stretch from the Canadian border to the tip of Florida. As a result, the climate varies considerably from the north, with its cold, snowy winters and short, warm summers, to the humid subtropical south. The rainfall is generally abundant, ranging from about 39 inches (100 cm) on the eastern coasts of Hokkaido to 150 inches (380 cm) on the highest mountains of Honshu.

Above: Mount Fuji, whose perfect cone soars 12,388 feet (3,776 m) above sea-level, is snow-capped all year round.

Below: Northern Japan has long, snowy winters. Conifers grow on sheltered mountain slopes.

The people

Japan's population was nearly 124,000,000 in 1991, making it the seventh most populous country in the world. By 2025 it is expected to be at a peak of 128,000,000 and then begin to decline very slowly. The continued growth of population is not because of a high birthrate, which has fallen by two-thirds since 1945, but because of a halving of the death rate resulting from improved living standards and health care. Japanese men can now expect to live to age 77, and women to 82. As a result, the proportion of old people in the population is growing rapidly.

The other remarkable feature of Japan's population is its sameness. Other nations of a similar size have significant numbers of citizens who differ from the majority in religion, language, or ethnic background. Japan does not. The major religious minority, Christians, number about 1.7 million. The major ethnic minority, Koreans, number around 690,000. The chief religion of Japan is Shinto – The Way of the Gods. It is based on a deep reverence for nature and teaches that every river, hill, and tree has its guardian spirit.

Above: A farmer's wife carries her baby high on her back, as Japanese have for centuries. But nowadays she probably has only one or two children, whereas her grandmother had five or six.

Left: Morning rush hour outside Tokyo's central station. More and more the Japanese are becoming a nation of office workers.

Above: An Ainu patriarch sits before the hearth in a traditional dwelling. The Ainu, the original inhabitants of Japan, have their own culture, religion, and language. There are now less than 20,000, all living in Hokkaido.

Right: Young Japanese illustrate a range of modern lifestyles – a soldier of the Ground Self-Defense Forces; a worker in an Osaka factory; Eiko Muromatsu, a well-known actress; and a young farmer from Honshu.

Below right: Dealers on the Tokyo Stock Exchange.

Other minorities include "Westerners" – North Americans and Europeans – who number about 60,000, or one in 2,000 of the population. The Ainu, the original inhabitants of Japan, number only about 20,000, all living on the island of Hokkaido.

Japan's remarkable cultural unity and the people's strong sense of identity as being Japanese is reinforced by an education system that ensures that everyone learns the same things the same way. For example, although there are regional accents and dialects, everyone understands the standard national form of the language used in education and broadcasting. Japanese, which is very different from the languages of its neighbors, Chinese and Korean, is spoken in no other country. This fact alone will probably ensure that Japan retains its distinctive character, however much it becomes "westernized."

Where people live

Because so much of Japan is mountainous, most people live on the narrow coastal plains. About 76 percent of the population lives in urban areas. In 1960, one-third of the people lived within 30 miles (50 km) of the center of one of the three biggest cities – Tokyo, Osaka, and Nagoya. By 1980 the proportion was nearer 42 percent. By the early 1990s, the trend was changing as more people moved out to suburbs or medium-size cities.

Urban life in Japan was traditionally associated with government. The first fixed capital was established at Nara in A.D. 710. In A.D. 794 the capital moved to nearby Kyoto, where it remained until 1868. Kyoto is still Japan's seventh largest city and a leading center for fashion, education, culture, and the arts.

Many other cities grew up as "castle towns" in which craftspeople and merchants gathered and settled to meet the needs of the samurai (the hereditary warrior class) who ruled the surrounding country from their fortresses. Many of these castles have been lovingly preserved or rebuilt.

Above: A farming village in Fuji's shadow. Living standards have risen in rural areas, and most homes are comfortable.

Below: A small town in Kyushu, with its many roadside signs, shows the American influence in modern Japan.

Left: A new housing estate. The price of well-spaced buildings is often a long journey to work in the city center.

Below: Crowded living conditions in central Tokyo. Houses, factories, and other buildings are mixed up together.

Several of Japan's major cities are little more than a century old. In 1853, when an American mission led by Commodore Matthew Perry demanded that Japan open its doors to foreign trade, Yokohama was just a small fishing village. Today it is a major commercial center of more than 3,000,000 people. Hokkaido's largest city, Sapporo, more than tripled in size between 1960 and 1990 - to about 1,663,000 people.

Other major population centers include the port of Kobe and the industrial areas of Fukuoka, Kitakyushu, and Kawasaki. Of course, millions of Japanese still live in small village communities in the mountains or on offshore islands. But, because of mass media and modern transportation, all have access to the comforts and conveniences of modern urban life. And, although a sense of regional identity is strong, the sense of national identity - of simply being Japanese - is stronger still.

Tokyo

Tokyo is a newcomer, compared with other world-class cities. Founded in 1457, it was chosen in 1590 by the warrior Ieyasu as the site for the capital of the regime he established. This was the Tokugawa shogunate (military dictatorship), which ruled Japan until 1868. Within a century, Tokyo – or Edo as it was then called – had nearly 1,000,000 people. In theory the capital was still at Kyoto, where the emperor lived, revered but powerless. But Edo, in practice, was the center of political life.

The revolution of 1868, which ended the rule of the Tokugawa in the name of the Emperor Meiji, also ended Kyoto's period as the nation's capital. Meiji took over Edo castle and renamed the city Tokyo – Eastern Capital. Burned down many times in the Edo period, Tokyo has continued to suffer disaster. In 1923 the Great Kanto Earthquake devastated the city and killed thousands of people. The Allied bombing raids in 1945 killed over 100,000. Today Tokyo sprawls once more over the Kanto plain, rebuilt twice in 50 years.

Above: Urban expressways relieve the intense pressure of traffic on the capital. Average weekday speed is only 7 mph (11 km/h).

Below: A plan of Tokyo, showing some of the most famous buildings, streets, and other features in this, one of the world's largest cities.

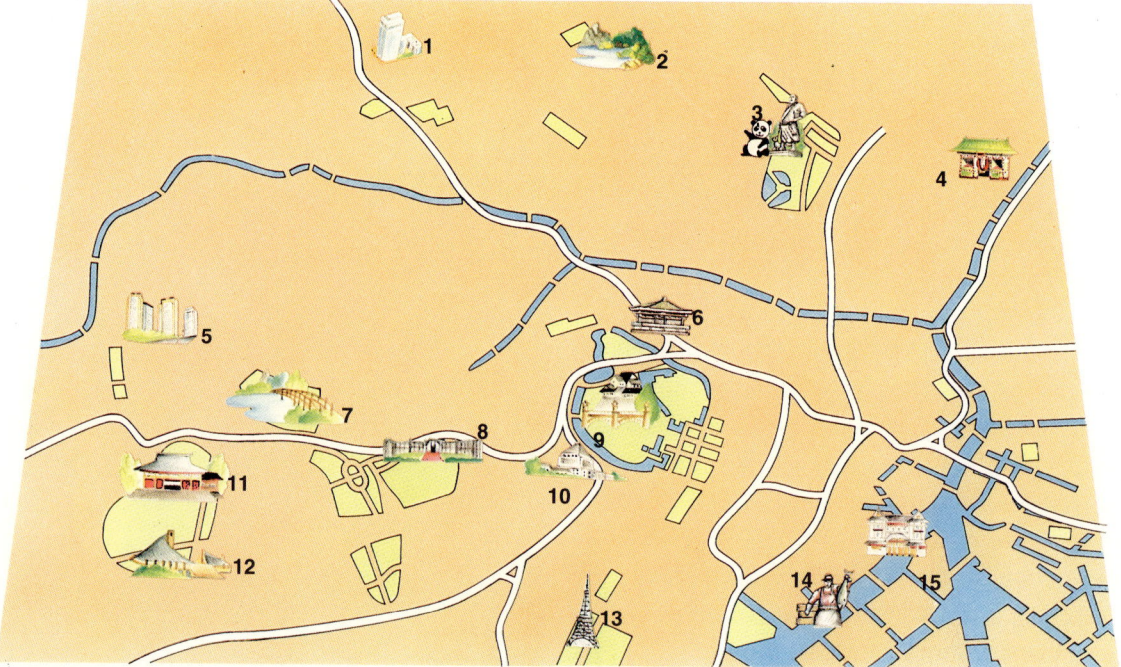

1 Sunshine and City Prince Hotel
2 Rikugien Gardens
3 Ueno Park
4 Asakusa Kannon
5 Tokyo Hilton International
6 Budokan Hall
7 Skinjuku Gyoen Garden
8 Akosaka Palace
9 Imperial Palace
10 National Diet
11 Meiji Shrine
12 Yoyogi Sports Center
13 Tokyo Tower
14 Central Wholesale Market
15 Kabukiza Theater

The commuting area of Tokyo embraces over 30,000,000 people, and Greater Tokyo officially includes about one-third as many. At the heart of the rebuilt city lies the Imperial Palace, surrounded by a majestic moat and park, separated from the bustle around it. To one side, near the old Tokyo railway station, lies Marunouchi, the central business district and home of the headquarters of all the major Japanese companies. On the other side lies Kasumigaseki, the government center and site of the National Diet (Parliament), Supreme Court and departments of state. Other distinctive areas include Roppongi, famed as an entertainment area, and Akasaka, a center for tourism and traditional crafts.

Few people, perhaps, would call Tokyo a beautiful city. But it has beautiful spots, such as Ueno Park and the impressive Meiji shrine. And it remains a bustling and exciting city – and one of the world's three great financial centers, along with New York City and London.

Above: The Imperial Palace, closed to all but courtiers and the most distinguished guests.

Below: Pedestrians on Ginza, where the official mint once stood, now famed for stores and bars.

Fact file: land and population

Key facts

Location: Japan is an archipelago, lying to the east of mainland Asia. Its main islands are situated roughly between latitudes 32° and 46° N and longitudes 129° and 147° E.

Main parts: Japan consists of four large islands - Honshu, Hokkaido, Kyushu, and Shikoku - which together make up more than 95 percent of the country. There are also about 3,900 smaller islands, including Okinawa in the Ryukyu chain (extending between Kyushu and Taiwan) and the Bonin Islands, which lie about 600 miles (970 km) to the southeast. The Northern Territories (the southern Kuril Islands) have been occupied by Russia since 1945, but they are still claimed by Japan. Japan is divided into 47 prefectures (the largest local government units).

Area: 145,841 sq miles (377,727 sq km).

Population: 124,460,000 (1992).

Capital: Tokyo.

Major cities (1991 populations):
- Tokyo (8,006,000)
- Yokohama (3,211,000)
- Osaka (2,512,000)
- Nagoya (2,098,000)
- Sapporo (1,663,000)
- Kobe (1,448,000)
- Kyoto (1,405,000)
- Fukuoka (1,193,000)
- Kawasaki (1,174,000)
- Hiroshima (1,062,000)
- Kitakyushu (1,020,000)
- Sendai (898,000)

Official language: Japanese. There are some regional differences in accent and everyday expressions, but everyone can speak and understand the standard Tokyo form of Japanese, which is used in schools and broadcasting.

Highest point: Mount Fuji, Honshu, 12,388 feet (3,776 m) above sea level. Mount Fuji is a dormant volcano that last erupted in 1707.

Longest river: Shinano-gawa, 228 miles (367 km). This river rises in the mountains of central Honshu and flows north into the Sea of Japan.

Largest lowland: Kanto Plain, around Tokyo, on Honshu.

Coastline: 9,936 miles (16,000 km).

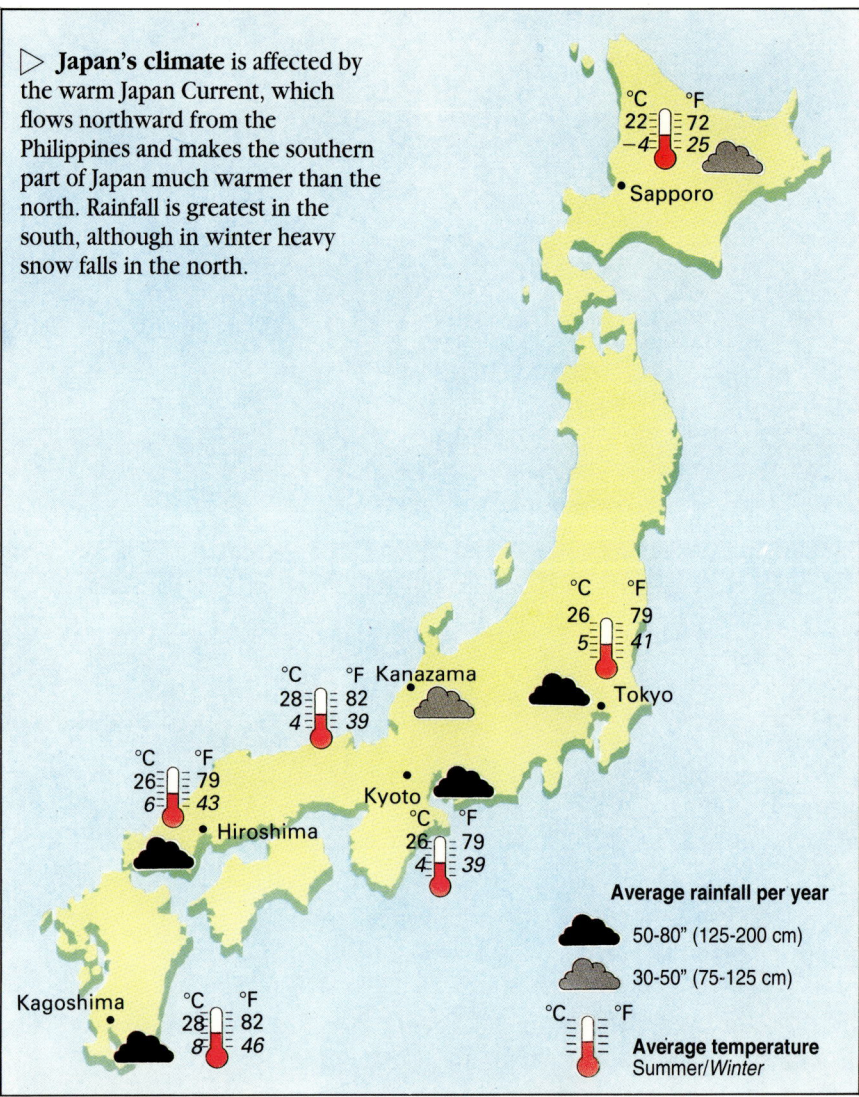

▷ **Japan's climate** is affected by the warm Japan Current, which flows northward from the Philippines and makes the southern part of Japan much warmer than the north. Rainfall is greatest in the south, although in winter heavy snow falls in the north.

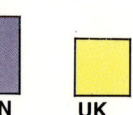

△ **A land area comparison**
Japan, with an area of 145,841 sq miles (377,727 sq km), is a small country in world terms. Britain, with 91,952 sq miles (229,880 sq km), is slightly smaller, whereas the United States is 25 times larger with 3,536,000 sq miles (9,194,000 sq km).

15

Australia 5 per sq mile (2 per sq km)

United States 70 per sq mile (27 per sq km)

◁ **A population density comparison**
Japan is one of the most densely populated countries in the world. Its population density is even higher than Britain's, and nearly 13 times as great as the United States'.

Britain 614 per sq mile (234 per sq km)

Japan 863 per sq mile (333 per sq km)

▽ **Where people live**
More than three-quarters of Japan's population is crowded into towns and cities, mostly on the coastal plains.

Cities and towns 77%   **Country** 23%

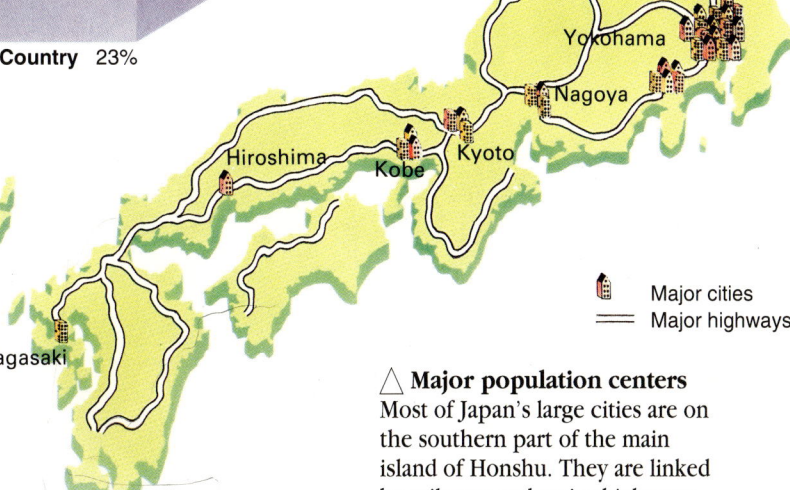

- Major cities
- Major highways

△ **Major population centers**
Most of Japan's large cities are on the southern part of the main island of Honshu. They are linked by railways and major highways, although ferries are important for travel between the islands.

Home life

Land is expensive in crowded Japan, and for this reason most homes are small. Overcrowding is worst in Tokyo, where more than one-third of the people consider that their homes are too small. The traditional Japanese house, still seen in rural areas, is built of wood and roofed with thatch or tiles. The "open plan" design, with sliding partitions of bamboo and paper, makes flexible use of space, so that rooms can be opened out for special occasions and outside walls removed in humid summers.

Major features of Japanese traditional interior design include rice-straw matting (*tatami*) as the floor-covering; the use of sliding-door wall cupboards for daytime storage of bedding and mattresses (*futon*), which are rolled out for use each night; and the presence of a *tokonoma*, or rectangular alcove, as the focal point of a room to display a painting or flower arrangement. Many modern Japanese homes still have at least one room with such traditional features.

Above: A traditionally dressed Kyushu family in their living room. Note the sliding screen opening onto the garden.

Below: A farming family from northern Honshu in their work clothes.

17

Left: Family meal in an apartment KD (kitchen-diner). Father is absent, as usual. Most men have long working hours and often get home late.

Below: Most children go to bed early, because schools start at about 8:00 a.m.

Japanese homes are well provided with electrical appliances; almost all have a refrigerator and a washing machine, and nearly two-thirds have air-conditioning. Family routines revolve around work and school. In major cities it is common for working parents and children to begin the day with a journey lasting an hour or more. Men usually leave early and often work late. On Sunday, the only certain day off work, families may go for a drive to the beach or the mountains. Vacations are usually taken as short, two- or three-day trips. Foreign travel is still an expensive luxury for most Japanese. It is reserved as a special treat for honeymooners or retirement couples.

A major responsibility of many Japanese women is to look after the home and family, in addition to working. This includes not only cooking and housework but keeping the family budget. In four-fifths of Japanese households, it is the woman who controls the family finances.

Stores and shopping

Japan has as many stores and shops as the United States, which has twice the population. With so many shops competing for business, the Japanese customer expects excellent service – and usually gets it. Surveys show that most Japanese women go shopping every day. Purchases of food and household goods are usually made from neighborhood shops, within walking distance of home. Because people buy daily from the same few stores, they are known and valued as customers. Sometimes a housewife may be reluctant to "shop around" for discounts, because this would look disloyal to the neighborhood.

Shops are major sources of jobs, especially for women. Shops, stores and the wholesalers who supply them with stock employ one in seven of the entire workforce. Because so many are family businesses, the spread of supermarkets has been prevented by the votes of the shopkeepers.

Above: A market trader, proud of the freshness of his produce. Notice the attention he pays to neat presentation.

Left: A typical street-scene in a city of a nation of shopkeepers.

Though Japan has few supermarkets, there are many department stores. The most famous is Mitsukoshi; other major *depatos* include Seibu and Takashimaya. Competition is just as intense between these large stores as between smaller shops. Many have art galleries and cultural exhibitions to attract customers. Another attraction is a "bargain basement" – but at the top of the building. As a result, customers have to pass through all the other floors to get to it – and usually see something to buy on the way.

A fashion-conscious, wealthy city, such as Kyoto, has many specialist shops, selling every variety of one single type of product, such as kimonos, neckties, confectionery, ceramics, or even combs. In Tokyo some of these cluster together to create specialized shopping areas, such as Kanda for books and Akihabara for electrical goods. Street markets still survive in Japan, not only in rural areas but also around famous shrines, at fishing ports, and wherever people are willing to pay a little more for fresh produce.

Above: Ancient and modern – these neon-lit booths line the main approach to the Asakusa temple, Tokyo. Booths like these, lit by lanterns, have been here for 300 years.

Below: A range of packaged foods and other items in a Japanese store. Convenience foods have become popular in recent years.

Cooking and eating

The traditional Japanese diet is one of the healthiest in the world – low in fats, high in fiber, and adequate in vitamins and minerals. Japan has one of the world's lowest rates of heart disease and one of the highest life expectancies. Rice still forms the core of most meals. Indeed, the Japanese word for breakfast literally means "first rice." When cooked, Japanese rice is slightly sticky – making it much easier to eat with chopsticks. It is also eaten cold as a picnic or snack dish. A favorite Japanese institution, increasingly popular overseas, is the *sushi* bar, where customers are served freshly made, bite-sized combinations of vinegared rice filled or topped with various kinds of seafood or pickle.

Fish and shellfish remain more important than meat as a source of dietary protein. Dairy products, such as milk, butter, and cheese, have become part of the normal family diet only since the 1950s and are much more popular with young people than with old.

Above: Stunning presentation makes every Japanese meal a special occasion.

Left: Guests in a Japanese hotel may be served elaborate meals in their rooms.

Left: A busy office canteen. Japanese tend not to linger over lunch but eat at leisure in the evenings.

Below: McDonald's – a highly successful importation. The customers consist almost entirely of young people.

Green tea (*o-cha*) is served with every meal – without milk or sugar. Coffee (*Kohii*) is another fairly recent import. Coffee shops provide a cheap meeting place for students and those out shopping. Sake, brewed from rice, is the traditional alcoholic drink for feasts and festivals. Nowadays, beer and whiskey are drunk more widely, especially by businessmen.

Entertaining in bars and restaurants is an important part of business life in Japan. Most men go out for drinks with colleagues and clients two or three nights a week, either to discuss problems in an easy atmosphere or simply to relax together. Many business people rely on professional caterers to supply box lunches for their office staff. Japan spends more on food and drink in the course of doing business than it does on national defense.

Housewives cook mostly for their children and themselves, except on Sundays, which is about the only time the whole family can be sure of sitting down at a meal all together.

Pastimes and sports

The most popular spectator sport in Japan is sumo, a unique and ancient form of wrestling. It requires the contestants to force their opponents either to step outside the straw-rope circle which marks the ring or to touch it with any part of the body – except the soles of the feet. Sumo has been a professional sport for at least 200 years and still involves much ritual as the wrestlers bow to referees and to each other, and "purify" the ring with salt. Fifteen-day contests are held six times a year and champions are hailed as national heroes.

Sumo may be little known outside Japan, but the same cannot be said of judo. Judo – which means "the supple way" – has developed from a form of unarmed combat to become a full-fledged international sport with Olympic status since Tokyo hosted the games in 1964. Another martial art which is rapidly gaining popularity round the world is kendo ("way of the sword") – a form of fencing that uses springy bamboo swords similar to those samurai swordsmen once used for practice.

Above: *Pachinko* – pinball – is Japan's most popular pastime after watching television.

Below: The sumo grand championships last fifteen days. Wrestling has been a professional sport for two centuries in Japan.

Among Western sports, the most popular are baseball, golf, tennis, and volleyball. Baseball was introduced by American missionaries more than 100 years ago and is played to the highest standard, both professionally and in the annual national high school contest. Golf has great prestige, especially among businessmen, but in crowded Japan space is expensive, so it can cost perhaps a year's salary just to join an exclusive club. Most people have to be content with a golf driving range. Tennis and volleyball, which can be played on small, hard-surfaced areas, are much better suited to city living in Japan.

Japan's mountains attract many people. Walking and climbing appeal to a few thousand enthusiasts, but skiing draws millions each winter. For the less hardy, there are traditional indoor pastimes and games. Origami, the art of paper-folding, has become popular in many countries. So has the board game "go," a contest of strategy in which players try to "capture" areas of "territory."

Above: Baseball is the most popular spectator sport after sumo wrestling.

Below: Gathering mussels at low tide. Shellfish have long been a delicacy in Japan and everyone can join in the hunt.

News and broadcasting

The Japanese are avid readers, with more than 100 daily newspapers to choose from. Five of these have both morning and evening editions, and among them account for about half of the total daily circulation: the *Yomiuri* (8.8 million), *Asahi* (nearly 8 million), *Mainichi* (nearly 5 million), *Nihon Keizai* (2.7 million) and *Sankei* (1.3 million). There are four English-language dailies: *The Japan Times*, *Asahi Evening News*, *Mainichi Daily News*, and *Daily Yomiuri*. Supplying them with news are the Kyodo News Service and Jiji Press.

Adding to this volume of print are more than 4,000 publishers, who among them produce more than 40,000 books a year and more than 3,000 magazines. Japan has one of the world's highest levels of newspaper readership. In 1989 newspaper circulation averaged about 584 copies per 1,000 people. Foreigners have often complained about the trade gap between Japan and other countries. Japan points to a news gap. They argue that the Japanese are far more knowledgeable about the rest of the world than the rest of the world is about Japan.

Above: Japan has over 99 percent literacy and the hunger for knowledge is strong. But these boys are probably flicking through *manga* – comic books.

Below: Some of the 3,000 magazines sold in Japan.

Above: About 50 million newspapers are sold each day.

Left: Comics have become very popular. Familiar characters such as Snow White and Mickey Mouse are to be found among Japanese ones.

Below: Specialist magazines, particularly popular with young people, cater for a wide range of interests.

Broadcasting began in 1925 with the Tokyo Broadcasting Station, later the *Nippon Hoso Kyokai* (Japan Broadcasting Corporation). NHK is an independent, nonprofit corporation financed by TV license fees. Its television service began in 1953, color transmissions were introduced in 1960, and stereo radio in 1978. Nowadays, 99 percent of Japanese homes have a color TV set, and only a very few communities in the mountains or on offshore islands cannot receive transmissions. Commercial broadcasting dates from 1950. There are seven major commercial channels and hundreds of radio stations. More than 100 million radios and 70 million television sets are in circulation.

While broadcasting flourishes, Japanese cinema is in relative decline. In 1960 there were more than a billion attendances: by 1990 there were only 146 million, and over two-thirds of the cinemas had closed.

Fact file: home life and leisure

Key facts

Population composition: In 1991, people under 15 years of age made up 18.0 percent of the population; people between 15 and 59 made up 64.3 percent; and people of 60 or over made up 17.7 percent. Women formed 50.9 percent of the population.

Average life expectancy at birth: 79.5 years in 1992, as compared with 72 years in 1970. (By comparison, people in the United States live, on average, 76 years and people in India 57.5 years.) In 1990, Japanese women had an average life expectancy of 82 years, as compared with 73 years in 1965. Women live, on average, six years longer than men.

Rate of population increase: Between 1965 and 1980, the population increased by about 1.2 percent a year. In 1980-1990, the rate was down to 0.6 percent. The rate is expected to fall gradually to 0.3 percent per year by 1989-2000, giving a population of about 128 million by the year 2000.

Family life: The average size of households in 1990 was 3.1.

Homes: In 1988, 64.0 percent of all Japanese homes were owner-occupied. The average annual income per household in 1989 was US $43,000 (as compared with $36,520 in the United States). Standards of living and public hygiene have increased greatly in Japan in recent years.

Work: In 1990, Japanese workers had an average working week of 39.5 hours. In 1990, the workforce totaled 63,840,000, of whom women made up 40.6 percent. In 1990, 2.1 percent of the workforce was unemployed. In 1990, about 25 percent of Japanese workers belonged to trade unions.

Prices: Prices rose sharply after the 1973 oil crises, reaching 31.6 percent in 1974. Inflation fell in the late 1970s and, between 1980 and 1990, the average inflation rate was down to 1.5 percent per year.

Religions: Most Japanese follow both Buddhism and Shintoism. Shintoism is a cult of reverence for nature. It is unique to Japan. Japan also has about 1,700,000 Christians.

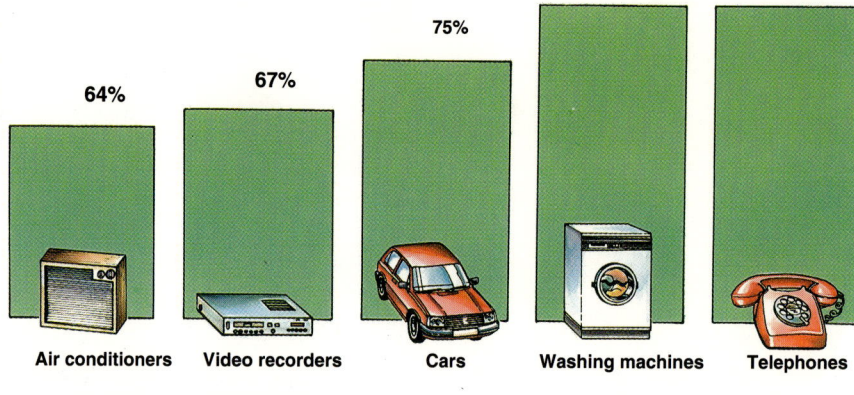

- Air conditioners 64%
- Video recorders 67%
- Cars 75%
- Washing machines 99%
- Telephones 99%

△ **How many households owned goods in 1989**
Nearly every Japanese household has a telephone and a washing machine, and television ownership is virtually 100%. Three out of every four households own a car.

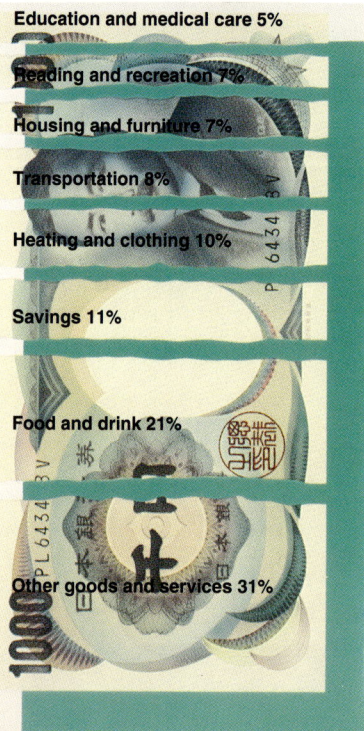

- Education and medical care 5%
- Reading and recreation 7%
- Housing and furniture 7%
- Transportation 8%
- Heating and clothing 10%
- Savings 11%
- Food and drink 21%
- Other goods and services 31%

◁ **How the average household budget is spent**
More than half the household budget is spent on food and other goods and services. After other costs have been met, the average family is still able to save a little over a tenth of its income.

▽ **Japanese currency**
The main unit of Japanese currency is the yen. Because of Japan's powerful economy, the yen is an international currency, and its rate of exchange with the U.S. dollar and the pound sterling is quoted on financial markets throughout the world.

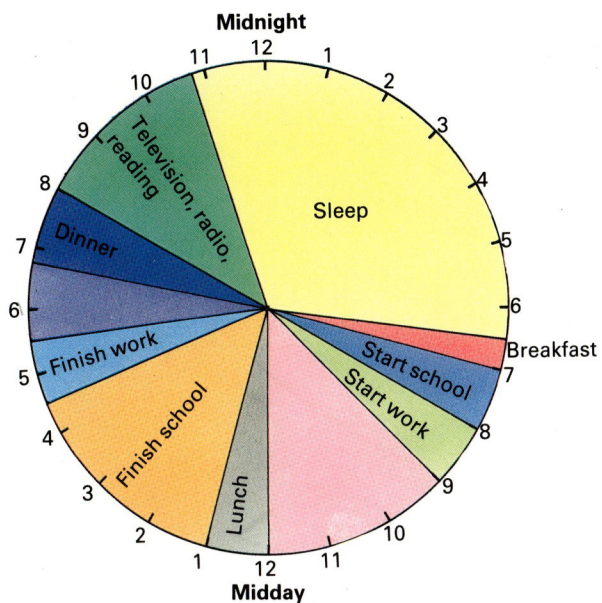

△ How the average family spends a working day

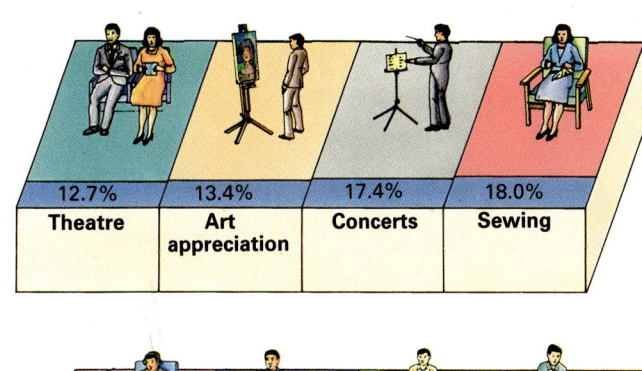

△ Popular leisure pursuits in Japan
Apart from practical activities such as handicrafts and gardening, most popular leisure pursuits in Japan are artistic in nature. Indeed, even gardening is regarded as an art by many people.

▽ Popular sports in Japan
In the late 1980s, about three out of every four people aged 15 or over took part in some kind of sport, with an emphasis on physical fitness. The most popular activity is jogging.

Skiing	Mountaineering Camping	Golf	Tennis	Volleyball	Cycling	Softball	Badminton	Table Tennis	Fishing	Swimming	Baseball	Jogging
11%	13%	14%	15%	15%	15%	20%	20%	20%	21%	24%	28%	30%

Farming and fishing

Japanese agriculture has been transformed since World War II. In the 1930s more than half of all workers were farmers. By 1990, the proportion had fallen to 7 percent. And whereas farmers had once been among the poorest people in Japan, their incomes are now above the national average. One reason for this is that 90 percent of farm households have another source of income, from building or work in an office or factory. Much of Japanese agriculture therefore relies on the labor of women and old people, while the men are away working elsewhere.

Because less than 15 percent of Japan's land area is suitable for agriculture, even steep hillsides are terraced for cultivation. Yet Japanese farms are very productive, despite their small average size of 3.3 acres (1.3 ha). Rice yields are among the highest in the world, and Japan produces enough meat for three-quarters of its needs. The secrets of success lie in the development of high-yielding, disease-resistant strains of crops and the widespread use of farm machinery, chemical fertilizers, and pesticides.

Above: A scene which recalls the past. Working horses are a rare sight nowadays in Japan.

Left: Mechanization has greatly raised rice farmers' productivity since 1945. The problem is now one of overproduction and surpluses.

29

Left: Picking mandarin oranges in southern Japan. Tariffs protect farmers from competition from imported Californian oranges.

Below: Japan's modern fishing fleet has been forced to fish farther and farther away from home waters because of local pollution problems.

Rice remains the most important single crop, but changes in the nation's diet have boosted the raising of livestock for meat, milk, and eggs, and the cultivation of a wider range of fruit and vegetables. Little can be spared for export. Agricultural products account for less than 1 percent of Japan's exports but 15.5 percent of its imports, chiefly cattle fodder, fish and shellfish, wheat, sugar, and soybeans.

Fish has traditionally been the major source of protein in Japan, and fishing remains a main source of both food and employment. About 450,000 vessels are registered as being professionally engaged in fishing. Coastal fish farming has developed to become a major branch of the industry. Despite the increasing amount of meat being eaten in Japan, fish products are still so important that Japan remains the world's greatest fishing nation in terms of volume of catch.

Industry

Japan has the second largest GNP (gross national product, or the total value of all goods and services) after the United States. Yet is has few natural resources and so minerals and other materials for industry have to be imported. Industry contributes 41 percent to the total value of Japan's GNP and employs about a quarter of the workforce.

Japan's iron and steel industry produces more than 100 million tons of steel each year, and two of the country's major industries are based on it: shipbuilding and car manufacture. Japan builds more ships and makes more cars than any other country. It also leads the world in the production of motorcycles and commercial vehicles. Each year, around 9 million cars, 3 million motorcycles, and 4 million commercial vehicles are produced. Industries based on electronics are also important to the Japanese economy. Again Japan is a world leader in the production of radios and television sets, and it also manufactures large numbers of video cameras and recorders, microcomputers, stereo equipment, and electronic calculators and watches.

Above: Shipbuilding was one of Japan's main industries until the 1970s, but has contracted because of Korean competition.

Below: Making refrigerators. Japanese electrical goods have won a worldwide reputation for quality and reliability.

Other domestic appliances manufactured in and exported by Japan include washing machines, refrigerators, and freezers. Japanese optical goods – particularly cameras and lenses – have an international reputation for quality.

The country also has a thriving chemical industry, whose chief products are plastics and synthetic fibers. A sizable proportion of the world's raw silk is produced in Japan, with 400,000 acres (160,000 ha) of land given over to the growing of mulberry trees, whose leaves are fed to silkworms.

Japan's industries consume large amounts of electricity, which is generated mainly in oil- or coal-burning power stations, although hydroelectricity (from dams on fast-flowing rivers) and nuclear power stations contribute more than a fifth of the total energy produced. Electricity is also the chief form of power used by Japan's railways.

Above: Japan is the world's leading producer and exporter of cars, motorcycles, and trucks.

Below: The electronics industry employs many young women.

Transportation

Japan's railways achieved world fame in 1964 with the establishment of the famed Bullet Train, which covered the 345 miles (555 km) between Tokyo and Osaka in just 3 hours 10 minutes. By 1975, this service had been extended via a tunnel to Hakata in Kyushu, 664 miles (1,069 km) from Tokyo. Another major development occurred in 1988 when the undersea Seikan Tunnel between Honshu and Hokkaido was opened to rail traffic. Railways are important in carrying passengers, but their share of freight traffic has fallen from nearly 40 percent in 1960 to about 7 percent in 1990.

Roads were rather neglected until 1954, when plans were made for a 5,000-mile (8,000-km) network of expressways. The first stretch, linking Kobe and Nagoya, opened in 1965 and the Tomei Expressway, a 216-mile (346-km) stretch from Tokyo to Nagoya, in 1969. The network is planned to be complete by the end of the century, when all four main islands should also be linked by bridges and tunnels.

Above: Rush hour subjects Tokyo's suburban railways to peak-loading and commuters are literally packed in.

Left: Speed, reliability, and luxury – the world-famous "Bullet Train" averages over 130 mph (200 km).

Road-building in Japan struggles to keep up with the ever-increasing volume of traffic. In 1965 there were fewer than 2,000,000 private cars in Japan. By 1990 there were more than 58,000,000. Also, although the expressways are built to the highest standard, only a third of the overall network is hard-surfaced.

In 1964 Japan's World War II losses had reduced its oceangoing fleet to just 17 ships. Nowadays Japan has the world's third largest merchant fleet after Liberia and Panama. The construction of such a massive fleet stimulated the steel industry, as well as the development of the country's many ports.

Progress in air transportation has been equally spectacular. Japan Air Lines (JAL) crossed the Pacific in 1954. By 1970, it was serving Paris and London. Japanese Air Lines was privatized in 1987. Japan's busiest airport is Tokyo International, or Haneda. Since 1978, Tokyo has also been served by the New Tokyo International Airport, also known as Narita, 38 miles (60 km) east of the capital city.

Above: A major highway interchange. But most roads are not adequate for the volume of traffic.

Below: Yokohama, now a major port, was just a fishing village little more than a century ago.

 34

Fact file: economy and trade

▽ **The distribution of economic activity in Japan**
Most industry is concentrated on the southern part of Honshu (the main island), whereas farming is important in the extreme south and north of the country.

🚢	Fishing port	⛏️	Mining
🍊	Mandarin oranges	🏭	Industry
🍇	Grapes and other fruit	🚢	Shipbuilding
🌾	Rice	🐄	Cattle

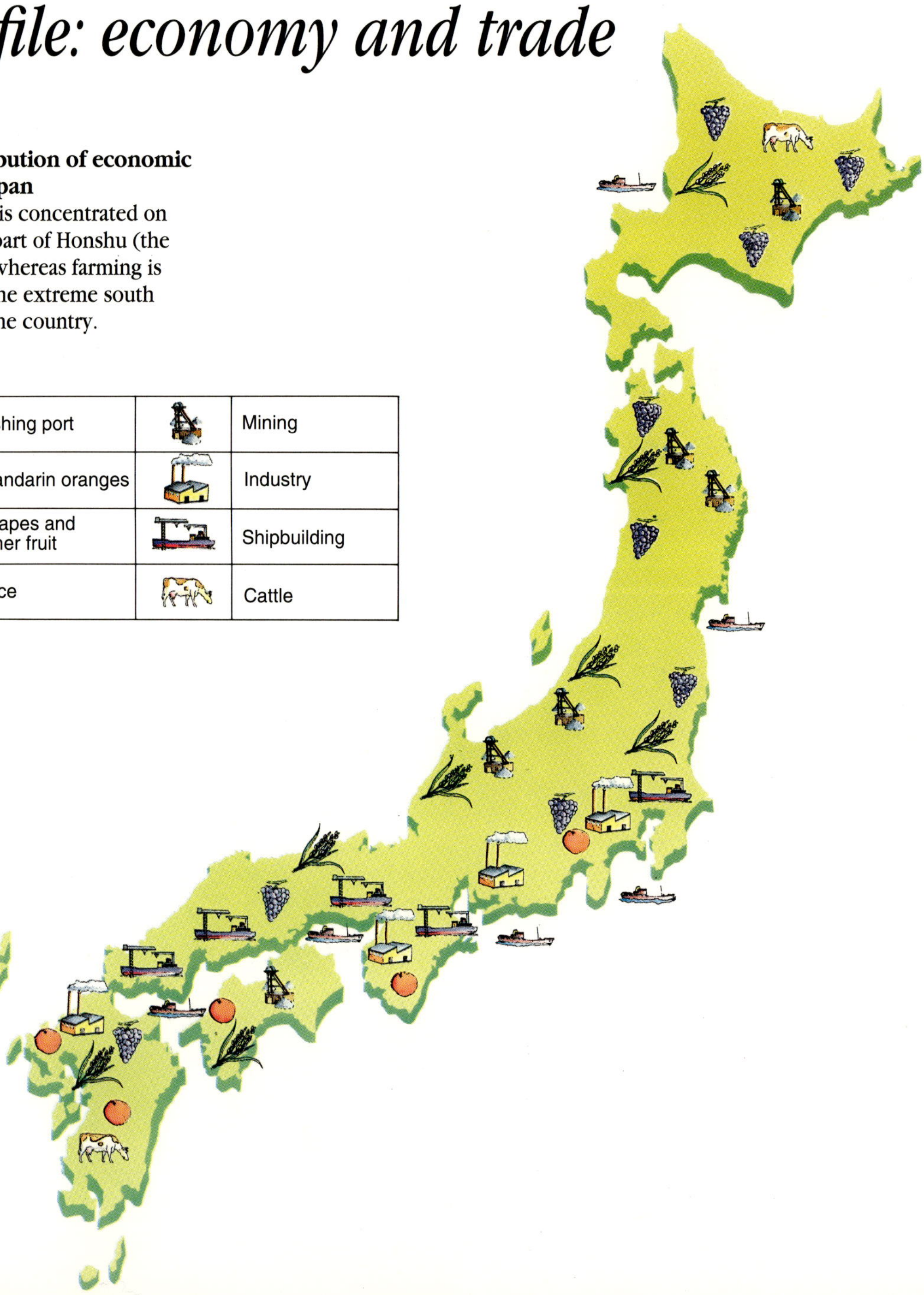

Key facts

Structure of production: Of the total gross domestic product (the GDP, or the value of all economic activity), farming, forestry, and fishing contribute 3 percent, industry 41 percent, and services 56 percent.
Farming: Farmland, including pasture, covers 14.5 percent of Japan. *Main products*: rice, vegetables (more than 40 varieties), fruits, dairy products.
Forestry: Forests cover 67.6 percent of the land.
Fishing: Japan is the world's leading fishing nation. It also leads in whaling.
Mining: Japan has some low-grade coal, but it imports all major minerals.
Energy: Japan imports most of the fossil fuels it needs to produce energy.
Manufacturing: Japan is the world's leading producer of motor vehicles, ships, and television sets.
Transportation: *Roads* (1990): 691,112 miles (1,114,697 km), used by 37,076,000 cars and 21,323,000 commercial vehicles; *Rail*: 17,059 miles (27,327 km); *Shipping*: the merchant fleet contains 7,568 vessels of 100 gross tons or more, including 1,164 oil tankers; *Air*: The main airlines are Japan Air Lines and All Nippon Airways.
Trade: (1991): *Total Imports*: US $236,737 million; *exports*: $314,525 million. Japan is the world's third trading nation.

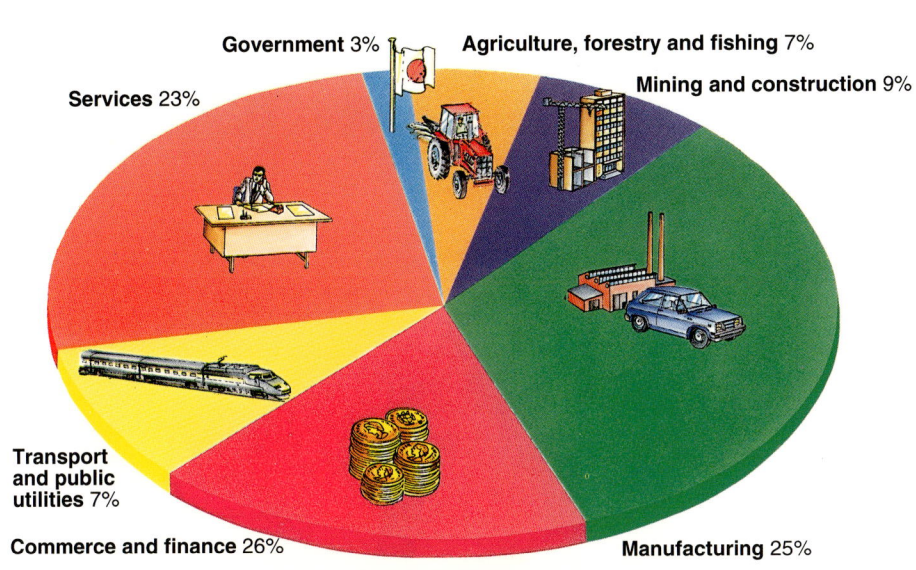

The distribution of employees by industry in 1990

In keeping with Japan's prosperous and growing economy, the service industries employ an increasingly large part of the total workforce.

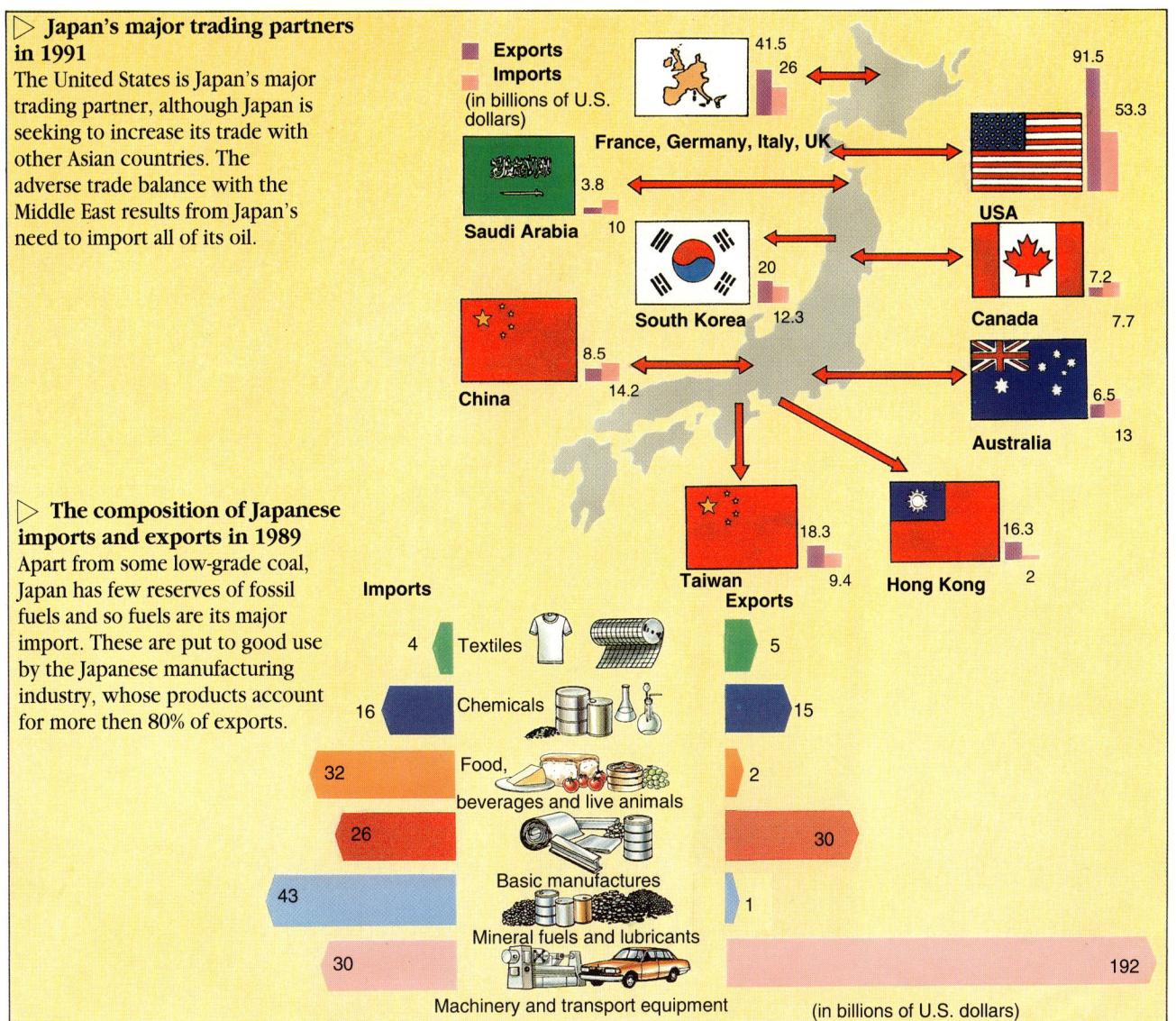

- Government 3%
- Agriculture, forestry and fishing 7%
- Mining and construction 9%
- Manufacturing 25%
- Commerce and finance 26%
- Transport and public utilities 7%
- Services 23%

Japan's major trading partners in 1991

The United States is Japan's major trading partner, although Japan is seeking to increase its trade with other Asian countries. The adverse trade balance with the Middle East results from Japan's need to import all of its oil.

Exports / Imports (in billions of U.S. dollars)

- France, Germany, Italy, UK: 41.5 / 26
- USA: 91.5 / 53.3
- Saudi Arabia: 3.8 / 10
- South Korea: 20 / 12.3
- Canada: 7.2 / 7.7
- China: 8.5 / 14.2
- Australia: 6.5 / 13
- Taiwan: 18.3 / 9.4
- Hong Kong: 16.3 / 2

The composition of Japanese imports and exports in 1989

Apart from some low-grade coal, Japan has few reserves of fossil fuels and so fuels are its major import. These are put to good use by the Japanese manufacturing industry, whose products account for more then 80% of exports.

Imports	Category	Exports
4	Textiles	5
16	Chemicals	15
32	Food, beverages and live animals	2
26	Basic manufactures	30
43	Mineral fuels and lubricants	1
30	Machinery and transport equipment	192

(in billions of U.S. dollars)

Education

Education in Japan is free and compulsory, and based on an American model, namely six years in elementary school, three years at junior high school, three more at senior high, and four years at college. The school starting age is six, but half of all children are already enrolled in a play group or kindergarten before that age. Compulsory schooling ends at 15, but 95 percent of all pupils complete senior high school and nearly 40 percent go on to a university or college.

Japanese schools teach a broad curriculum of nine or ten subjects right through to college-entrance level. The Ministry of Education gives detailed guidelines for every subject and approves all textbooks. The Japanese language is a major study; despite the difficulty of writing the system, there are virtually no illiterate people in Japan. International tests also show that the average levels of achievement in mathematics are much higher than in the United States or Britain.

Above: A primary school class on a trip. Bright hats help teachers keep an eye on the children.

Below: Morning school assembly takes place in the playground during the summer.

Art, physical education, music, and science are also studied, and pupils get an extra chance to extend their skills in these areas through after-school clubs, held daily. The school week includes Saturday, and pupils have lots of homework as well as holiday projects. Competition is tough and about half of all high school pupils also go to *juku*, and evening cramming school, to help them keep up. Parents have to pay for *juku*. Some parents and teachers worry that the pressure for success can create such problems as bullying and even suicide. But everyone agrees that it is essential to get the best possible education. It is almost impossible to get a good job without a high school diploma. Ambitious students, aiming for a job with a famous big company, have to be accepted at one of the top universities. Only about 20 percent receive scholarships. The rest have to rely on their parents to pay for them. Japan's only real resource is its people, which explains why education is given such a high priority.

Above: A Japanese language lesson in elementary school, where most of the teachers are women.

Below: Junior high school students in summer uniform wait to greet a group of visiting British teachers.

Traditional Japan

Japan's modern products are renowned throughout the world for quality and reliability. One reason for this is the long tradition of craftsmanship that lies behind them. To maintain this tradition, the Japanese have a system of rewarding outstanding potters, weavers, or wood-carvers as "Living National Treasures." Modern Japanese consumers are still eager to buy their products, and ancient cities – such as Kyoto and Kamakura – are still major centers of traditional production.

Perhaps the most famous of Japan's traditional products are the swords of the samurai. Japanese swordsmiths regarded their work as a sacred task and used Shinto rituals to purify themselves and the smithy before beginning work. The swords they made were a clever combination of soft and hard steels. Soft steel alone would have given weight and strength but a dull cutting edge. Hard steel alone would have shattered in combat.

Above: A samurai sharpens a treasured blade. Sword-making was traditionally the most exalted of all crafts.

Left: Young women, called geisha, are trained from childhood in the arts of conversation, music, and dance. Here, they offer refreshment to a guest. Geisha are renowned for their skill in entertaining.

If swords are found now only in museums, lacquer-ware can be seen everywhere in homes and restaurants. The Japanese learned from China how to use the natural resin of the lacquer tree to varnish wooden bowls and boxes to preserve and decorate them. Silk manufacture was another art learned from China in which the Japanese came to excel their teachers, especially in the arts of dyeing and hand-painting. Ceramics are also traditional products still in daily use. Most restaurants have tableware designed specially for them.

With a true appreciation of the qualities of the materials they use, Japanese craftspeople have displayed amazing versatility with paper and bamboo, using paper to make lanterns and sliding screens, and bamboo for such diverse objects as water pipes, flutes, fences, baskets, practice swords, and whisks for the tea ceremony. The tea ceremony is the visitor's best chance to see fine craft goods, including utensils of pottery, lacquer, metal, cloth, and bamboo, all in graceful use.

Above left: Flower-arranging, called *ikebana*, is a traditional art which arose from offering flowers to the gods.

Above: A geisha applying makeup. The word geisha means "art person."

Below: A dazzling display of folding fans. In humid summer, a fan is not only an attractive fashion accessory but a practical necessity.

The arts

The Japanese have a deep love of art, respect for artists, and a desire to honor both in their everyday lives. Art galleries and exhibitions attract large crowds. There are numerous schools and independent teachers to give instruction. And big companies try to gain prestige by buying famous works of art for their offices. Even the samurai, Japan's traditional warrior class, were great patrons of the arts and took great pride in such accomplishments as the tea ceremony and calligraphy. Calligraphy, written in various scripts, is perhaps the most valued of all art forms.

The allied art of painting has drawn its inspiration from nature, from court life, and from the lives of the common people. Japanese artists pioneered the multicolor wood-block print that depicted the women, theaters, and other delights of the "floating world" of the pleasure districts of Edo and Kyoto. Like much of Japanese poetry, these prints suggest that beauty, like pleasure, is always fleeting.

Above: Women are a favorite subject of Japanese wood-block prints.

Left: The best-known print from Hokusai's celebrated series "36 Views of Mount Fuji."

Above: Scene from a Kabuki play, in which all parts are played by men.

Below: Hotei, a lucky god, finely carved in ivory.

Later artists, such as Hokusai (1760-1849) and Hiroshige (1797-1858), developed the prints as a means of depicting landscapes. Sculpture in Japan was long influenced by Buddhism, introduced from China in the sixth century A.D. Buddhist temples still contain outstanding examples of figures of the Buddha and Buddhist saints and demons. The Japanese consider flower arranging (*ikebana*) and the cultivation of miniature trees (*bonsai*) high art activities, which in the West might be considered merely pastimes.

Japanese tastes in music are wide ranging. Tokyo supports many Western-style symphony orchestras, and some 600,000 people a year enter the music examinations of the Yamaha company. But there is also a great interest in learning such traditional instruments as the *shamisen* (a sort of three-stringed lute), *koto* (a type of harp) and the *shakuhachi* (a flute). Drama shows a similar mixture of Western and traditional forms, such as *Noh* (masked), *Bunraku* (puppet), and *Kabuki* (costumed).

The making of modern Japan

Until 1853, Japan cut itself off from the rest of the world, apart from a trickle of trade through Dutch and Chinese merchants. Then a U.S. war fleet led by Commodore Matthew Perry demanded that Japan open its ports.

After a period of political confusion, a group of young samurai seized power in the name of the Emperor Meiji in 1868. To save Japan from becoming a Western colony they pushed through a program of reform which transformed it into a major industrial and military power. Japan was strong enough to defeat China in 1894-95 and Russia in 1904-5 to gain control of Korea, which became a Japanese colony in 1910.

But relations with the West began to turn sour when the United States banned Japanese immigrants in 1924. The collapse of world trade after 1929 hit Japan hard. Because its politicians seemed unable to find an answer to Japan's problems, the army took the lead and began to conquer East Asia, as an outlet for Japanese trade and migration.

Above: An 18th-century painting of a 12th-century warrior. The Japanese have long had a strong sense of the past.

Below left: A 16th-century screen depicts foreign visitors.

Below: The American Commodore Matthew Perry.

In 1937 Japan began a full-scale war in China, ignoring United States pressure to pull back. In 1941 a Japanese task force attacked the American base at Pearl Harbor, Hawaii, while Japanese troops swept through Southeast Asia as far as the borders of India. The combined strength of the Allies finally pushed Japan out of all its conquests, and in August 1945 the dropping of atomic bombs on Hiroshima and Nagasaki forced Japan to surrender.

From 1945 to 1952, Japan was occupied by American troops. Democratic reforms gave votes to women, land to farmers, and the right to form unions to workers. By 1955, with substantial aid from the United States, Japan's economy had recovered from wartime losses, and during the 1960s it grew by 10 percent each year. By the 1980s, Japan had begun to emerge as a major power in world finance and a world leader in high-technology industries, such as computers and robotics.

Above: A naval action of the Russo-Japanese war. Japan's victory astonished the Western powers.

Below: After the bomb at Hiroshima. Only the few steel and concrete structures survived the blast and fire storm.

Japan in the modern world

Japan is a country of paradoxes. Its economy puts it in the top league with the United States and Germany, but it has very little military power.

Its people enjoy a high standard of living, yet Japan has almost no resources. Japanese brand names are known around the world, yet few besides experts could name even half a dozen of its people. Japanese technology is transforming the lives of people everywhere, though its inventors have won few Nobel prizes. Few countries have so distinct a national culture, yet many Japanese gifts to the world are scarcely recognized as such. Judo, instant noodles, and space invader games all come from Japan but few know them as Japanese.

More and more the people of the world look to Japan to play a greater role in international affairs. Japan has responded by greatly increasing its aid to developing countries, sending money, technical assistance, and personnel. Contacts with the rest of Asia are increasing. Between 1985 and 1991, Japan's exports to eastern Asian countries tripled.

Above: Hiroshima today, a thriving city but mindful of its past.

Below left: Limbering up before the morning shift. Many Western companies admire Japanese work methods.

Below: The Tokyo Stock Exchange, with those in London and New York, is one of the three most important world financial centers.

Left: Emperor Akihito and his wife, Empress Michiko.

Below: A Japanese survey rocket blasts off. Japan is in the forefront of technology, including rocketry, electronics, and computers.

Above: Japanese people are living longer and the proportion of retired people is increasing rapidly.

Japan is hampered by a language barrier. Not only does no other nation speak Japanese, but the Japanese themselves find learning other languages difficult. A recent survey suggested that fewer than one in six of Japan's high school teachers of English could actually hold a real conversation in the language. But this is scarcely surprising when fewer than 1 percent have ever had the chance to live in an English-speaking country.

This fact reflects the paradox of Japan's isolation. Japan exports its products throughout the world, but fewer than 5 percent of its people have passports. The typical Japanese, outside the big cities, has never met a foreigner from the West. Yet this is changing slowly. Almost 700,000 Japanese now live overseas as businessmen, diplomats, or students. In Britain, Japanese-run factories cluster together in such industrial areas as South Wales and the Northeast. Contacts are increasing at all levels.

Fact file: government and world role

Key facts

Official name: Japan. The Japanese call their country Nippon or Nihon.

Flag: A circular red disk on a white ground.

National anthem: Kimigayo (The Reign of Our Emperor).

National government: Japan is a constitutional monarchy, with the Emperor as "symbol of the state." The three branches of government are the executive, legislative, and judicial. The Diet (parliament) has two houses, the 512-member House of Representatives and the House of Councillors, which has 100 members, who between them represent the whole of Japan, and 152 members from the prefectures. The chief executive of government is the Prime Minister, selected from among members of the Diet. The Prime Minister heads the cabinet, more than half of whose members must be drawn from the Diet. Judicial power is vested in the Supreme Court, consisting of the Chief Justice (appointed by the Cabinet) and 14 other judges. The Supreme Court has eight regional high courts, 50 district courts, and various local and family courts.

Local government: Local administration is in the hands of 47 prefectures, each with a governor and an assembly. In addition, each of the approximately 500 cities, 2,000 towns, and 800 villages elects a mayor and one-house assembly.

Defense: Constitutionally, Japan can have no armed forces, so there is no national army, navy, or air force. There are, however, "Self-Defense Forces" divided among Ground (150,200 members in 1992, plus 46,000 reservists); Maritime (44,000); and Air (46,400).

International organizations: Japan is a member of various international organizations. It became a member of the United Nations in 1956 and it belongs to the International Monetary Fund and various United Nations agencies. Japan also belongs to the Organization for Economic Co-operation and Development (OECD), the Asian Development Bank, the Asian and Pacific Council, and the Colombo Plan.

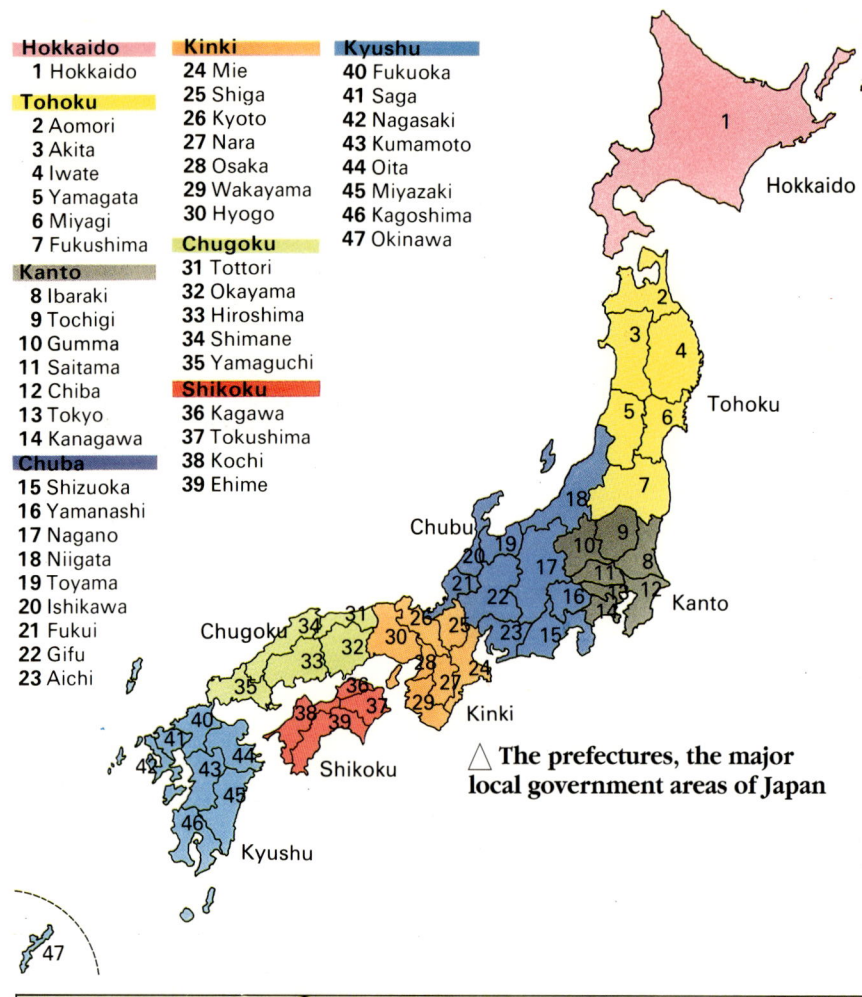

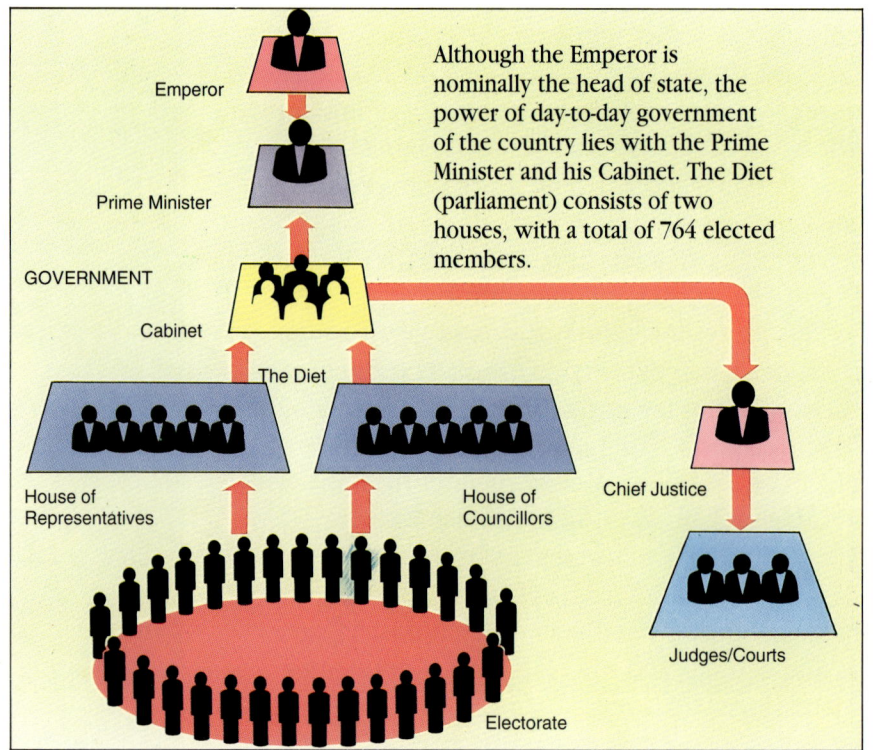

Hokkaido
1 Hokkaido

Tohoku
2 Aomori
3 Akita
4 Iwate
5 Yamagata
6 Miyagi
7 Fukushima

Kanto
8 Ibaraki
9 Tochigi
10 Gumma
11 Saitama
12 Chiba
13 Tokyo
14 Kanagawa

Chuba
15 Shizuoka
16 Yamanashi
17 Nagano
18 Niigata
19 Toyama
20 Ishikawa
21 Fukui
22 Gifu
23 Aichi

Kinki
24 Mie
25 Shiga
26 Kyoto
27 Nara
28 Osaka
29 Wakayama
30 Hyogo

Chugoku
31 Tottori
32 Okayama
33 Hiroshima
34 Shimane
35 Yamaguchi

Shikoku
36 Kagawa
37 Tokushima
38 Kochi
39 Ehime

Kyushu
40 Fukuoka
41 Saga
42 Nagasaki
43 Kumamoto
44 Oita
45 Miyazaki
46 Kagoshima
47 Okinawa

△ The prefectures, the major local government areas of Japan

Although the Emperor is nominally the head of state, the power of day-to-day government of the country lies with the Prime Minister and his Cabinet. The Diet (parliament) consists of two houses, with a total of 764 elected members.

Emperor
Prime Minister
GOVERNMENT
Cabinet
The Diet
House of Representatives
House of Councillors
Chief Justice
Judges/Courts
Electorate

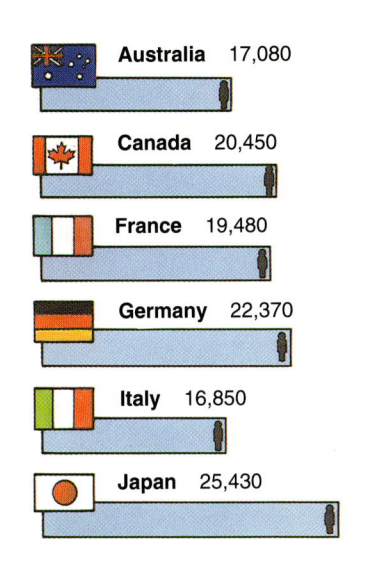

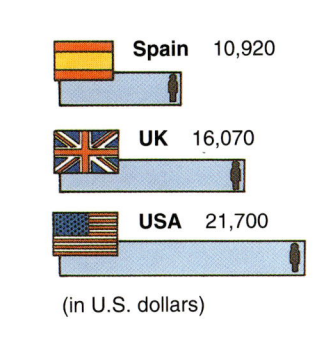

Country	Wealth (US$)
Australia	17,080
Canada	20,450
France	19,480
Germany	22,370
Italy	16,850
Japan	25,430
Spain	10,920
UK	16,070
USA	21,700

(in U.S. dollars)

◁ **National wealth created per person in 1990**
Japan is a wealthy nation, and individual contributions to the economy are greater only in the United States and Canada.

▽ **Preferred international partners**
When asked in an opinion poll which nation they would prefer to maintain closest relations with, most Japanese people favored the United States. But more than a fifth of those interviewed wanted to increase contact with other Asian countries, particularly China and South Korea, Japan's nearest neighbors.

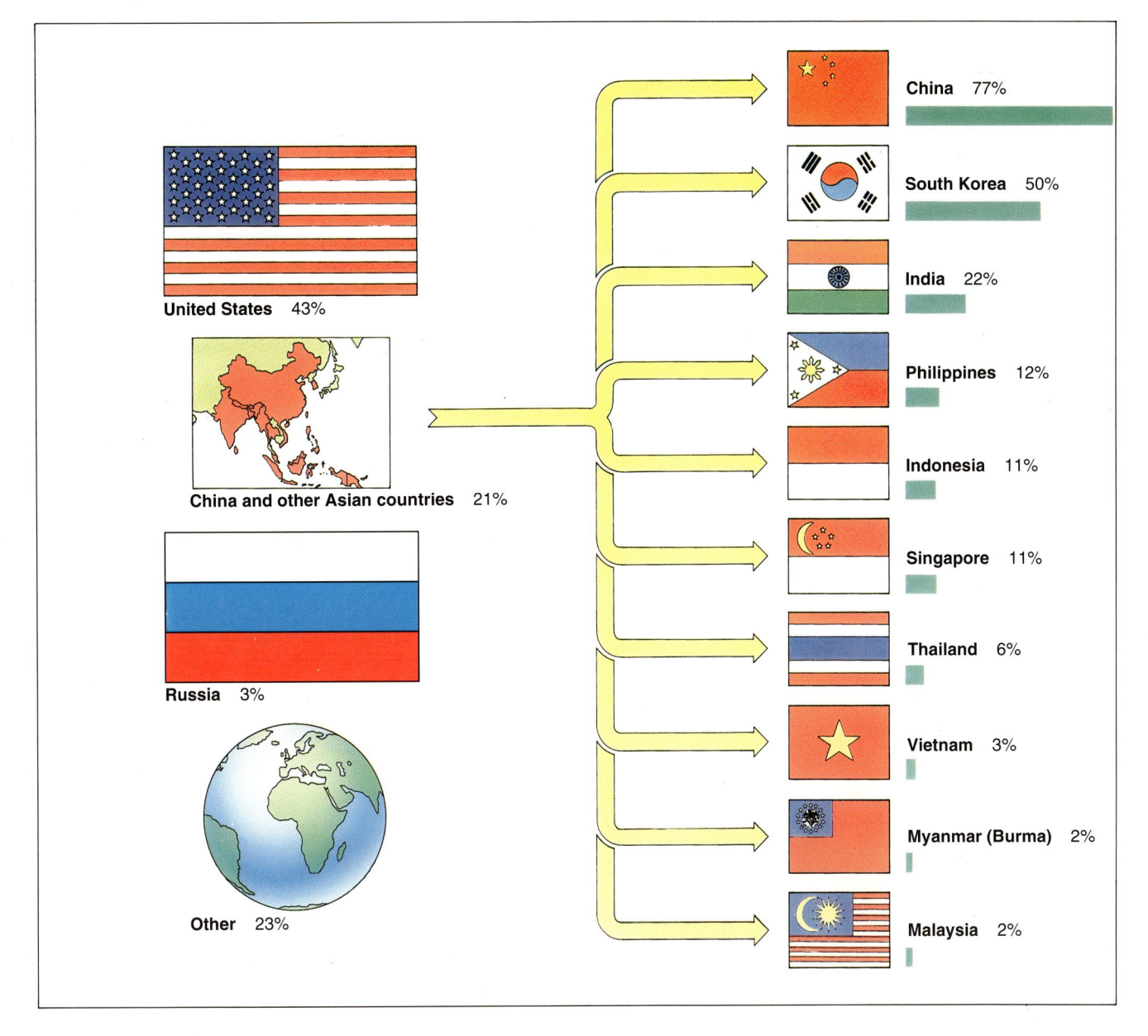

- United States 43%
- China and other Asian countries 21%
- Russia 3%
- Other 23%

- China 77%
- South Korea 50%
- India 22%
- Philippines 12%
- Indonesia 11%
- Singapore 11%
- Thailand 6%
- Vietnam 3%
- Myanmar (Burma) 2%
- Malaysia 2%

Index

Agriculture 28-29
Ainu 9
Air transport 33, 34
Akasaka 13
Akihito, Emperor 45
American occupation 43
Armed forces 46
Arts 40-41
Atomic bomb 43

Bamboo 16, 31
Baseball 23
Birthrate 8
Bombing 12
Bonin Islands 5, 7
Bonsai 41
Books 24
Broadcasting 25
Buddhism 26, 41
Bullet Train 32
Bunraku 41
Business 21, 45

Calligraphy 40
Cars 33
Castle towns 10
Cattle 34
Ceramics 31
China, war with 42
Christians 8, 26
Climate 7
Coal 34
Colleges 36
Computers 31, 43
Cooking 20-21
Courts 46
Crops 28

Death rate 8
Department stores 19
Diet (Parliament) 13, 46
Divorce 26
Drama 41

Earthquakes 6, 12
Economy 5, 34, 43, 44
Edo 12, 40
Education 9, 36-37
Electricity supply 34
Energy 34
Entertainment 24-25

Farming 28 -29, 34
Films 25
Fish farming 29
Fishing 29, 34
Flower arranging 41
Forestry 34
Fujiyama. *See* Mount Fuji
Fukuoka 11, 14
Futon 16

Geisha 38-39
Golf 21, 23
Government 10, 46

Hakata 32
Health care 8
Hiroshige 41
Hiroshima 14, 43, 44
Hokkaido 5, 7, 9
Hokusai 41
Homes 16-17, 26
Honshu 5, 6, 7
Hydroelectricity 34

Ieyasu 12
Ikebana 41
Imperial Palace 13
Industry 30-31
Islands 7, 14

Judo 22, 44
Juku 37

Kabuki 41
Kamakura 30
Kanto plain 7, 14
Kasumigaseki 13
Kawasaki 11, 14
Kendo 22
Kindergarten 36
Kitakyushu 11, 14
Kobe 11, 14, 32
Korea 42
Koreans 8
Kuril Islands 14
Kyoto 10, 12, 14, 19, 30, 40
Kyushu 5

Lacquer-ware 39
Landscape 6-7, 14
Language 9, 14, 36, 45
Life expectancy 26
Livestock 34

Magazines 24
Manufacturing 34
Markets 19
Martial arts 22
Marunouchi 13
Marriage 26
Meiji 13, 42
Mining 34
Miyazawa, Kiichi 45
Mountain climbing 23
Mountains 6
Mount Fuji 6, 14
Music 41

Nagasaki 43
Nagoya 10, 14, 32
Nara 10
Newspapers 24
Nippon 46
Noh 41
Nuclear power 34

Okinawa 7

Origami 23
Osaka 10, 14, 32

Painting 40
Parliament 13
Pastimes 22-23
Pearl Harbor 43
People 8-9, 11
Perry, Matthew 11, 42
Population 8-9, 14, 15, 26
Ports 33
Pottery 39
Prices 26
Publishing 24

Radio 25
Rail transport 32, 34
Rainfall 7
Religion 8, 26
Rice 20, 28, 34
Rivers 7
Roads 32-33, 34
Roppongi 13
Russia, war with 42
Ryukyu Islands 5, 7

Sakai 14
Sake 21
Samurai 10, 30, 40, 42
Sapporo 11, 14
Schools 36-37
Sculpture 41
Shikoku 5
Shinanao-gawa 14
Shinto 8, 26
Ships 33, 34
Shopping 18-19
Silk 31
Skiing 23
Sports 22-23
Stores 18-19
Students 37, 44
Sushi 20
Sumo 22
Swords 30

Tatami 16
Tea ceremony 39
Technology 30-31, 44
Television 25
Tennis 23
Timber 34
Tokonoma 16
Tokugawa 12
Tokyo 6, 10, 12-13, 14, 16, 19, 32, 45
Trade 34
Transportation 32-33
Tsunami 6

Unemployment 26
United States 42
University 36

Vacations 17

Volcanoes 6
Volleyball 23

Westernization 9
Wood-block prints 40
Workforce 26
Working week 26
World War II 33, 43

Yokohama 11, 14